Oh, Yes I I Can!

written by

Michael T.

illustrated by

Joe Santoro

A Children's Book About Career Choices

Oh, Yes I Can!

Published by Acorn Book Services

For information call: 304-279-2858
or Email: acornbookservices@gmail.com

Designed by Acorn Book Services
Publication Managed by Acorn Book Services
www.acornbooksesrvices.com
acornbookservices@gmail.com
304-995-1295

Photography by Charly: 304-886-4318

ISBN-13: 978-1492209645
ISBN-10: 1492209643

In memory of Gilbert T. Myers,
who could do everything.
Thanks, Dad, for your great example.
I miss you!

"Joe and Michael T. have created a wonderful introduction to the world of careers for young readers. A variety of occupations are woven into this beautifully illustrated book with clever rhyming text. Perfect for parents, teachers, school counselors, and anyone who wants to entertain and open the minds of our youth."

Tricia. B. Ballard
Elementary School Counselor
10 years

Oh, Yes I Can!

written by

Michael T.

illustrated by

Joe Santoro

A Children's Book About Career Choices

"I can do all things through Christ who strengthens me."

Philippians 4:13

Mikey was a dreamer
Deciding what to be.
Not really that important
When he was only three.

But as the years passed him by
His thoughts were never clear
On what to be or become
He knew he must not fear.

Perhaps a good mechanic
So he could change some tires,
Or how about a fireman
So he could help fight fires?

9

An officer of the law
Take crime off of the streets.
Working in the food market
Stock produce and fresh meats.

Growing fruits and vegetables
Way out upon the farm,
Or he could be a healer
Who helps and never harms.

Speaking about the Bible,
He would be a preacher.
Sharing words in school to learn
We must call him Teacher.

Mikey thinks as days go by,
What is it he could be?
Many choices to pick from
Like fishes in the sea.

13

A fisherman, that's a choice!
Set sail in his large boat.
Maybe a politician
For whom we cast our vote.

14

Meanwhile at the restaurant
Guy who takes our orders,
Or the guard who watches for
Safety at our borders.

Sanitation, it is good
He's the trash collector,
Or business man we might call
Boss or our director.

The builder who builds it right
Heavy brick and mortar,
To the man who walks the train;
He's the helpful porter.

Serviceman in other lands
Who helps to keep us free,
Or the one who climbs so high
To cut and trim those trees.

Lots of tricks and animals
Call him the magic man.
Mikey knows think positive
And always say, "I Can."

19

A pilot high in the sky
Flying from town to town.
He could entertain the kids
By posing as a clown.

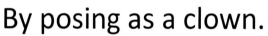

Mikey loves all kinds of sports:
Baseball, football, soccer,
Tennis, golf and b-ball too,
He could be a boxer.

On the highways day and night
Driver of big rigs.
History and dinosaurs
Create the new dirt digs.

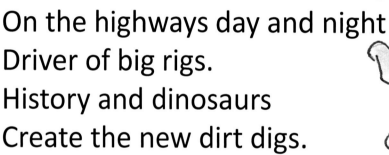

He may like to eat and taste,
Ice cream flavor tester.
He could walk right through the swamp
Alligator wrestler.

How 'bout a wild west cowboy
Instructing a line dance,
Or teach Ol' Santa's reindeer
To walk now with a prance.

Send some things to outer space
Launching helpful rockets.
Acting in a tour on stage
Playing Davy Crockett.

Take a picture on the wall
Around it build a frame.
Great idea for family night
Create a new board game.

26

Mikey calls for highest bid
Just like an auctioneer.
Making little people talk
He'd be a puppeteer.

All kinds of jobs he could dream
And even try his hand
Big thinking in America
This is the promise land!

28

All these persons he could be
When Mikey is a man,
Lots of hard work and belief
And saying, "Yes I Can!"

29

So stay in school, learn even more
And always take your stand.
When others tell you that you can't
Just shout, "Oh, Yes I Can!"

Mikey's Project Page

Parents and Teachers: After reading about all of the occupations (jobs) that Mikey could have when he grows up; discuss the ones that might be the most fun, the hardest to work, the most rewarding, and the one they would like to do.

See how many jobs they can remember and make a list on paper or on the board. This scratches their memory and expands their minds.

Now, have each child/student draw on a separate sheet of paper the one occupation they would like to be when they grow up. Encourage details like the farmer is carrying fruits or vegetables or milking cows or plowing a field on a tractor; the fire fighter is driving a fire truck, or holding a fire hose or an ax or rescuing a person or animal. The more details, the more you have the opportunity to correct misconceptions about the occupation and reward valid thoughts of the job.

See how many occupations the children/students can name that are not in the book. You will be amazed at the ones they will come up with. In fact, perhaps another project would be to draw a picture of their parents' type of work. That should be an eye-opener of their perception. Have fun!

Mikey would enjoy seeing everyone's artwork. You can send it to:

Michael T. and Mikey
P.O. Box 2955
Martinsburg, WV 25402

Photocopy This Page

"OH YES I CAN" word search

```
A I T S T A U A Z U T F U L A B B T H
L C N E D F G C K S C M W B D U M G K
L A U R I B A T D C A U Q E B S N X V
I N M V P T M O R H V J P L W I Z D A
G Y A I U E E R O O C Y R I A N M I F
A V G C P A R D C O O E E A M E N O I
T H I E P C F M K L W U A F E S C N S
O A C M E H I P E W B P C W R S H O H
R U I A T E R O T O O P O H Q I M A E
E C A N T R E L S R Y L E Z C A N U R
I T N T E F M I E K S I R B A N I R M
D O Z S D R N E V R O I T R G P C S A
E N D T C M N M E I R C R E R P B U N
E E O E L E P A R M T I U A O O I R T
R E C R O R I N N M S A C M C R L M Q
M R T M W U L U G E Y N K E E T D E F
M Y O F N Z O E B R L P E R R E E R J
C A R V J C T R U C G S R J S R R U X
```

ACTOR	FRAMER	SERVER
ALLIGATOR	GAMER	SERVICEMAN
AMERICA	GROCER	SPORTS
AUCTIONEER	ICAN	TEACHER
BELIEF	MAGICIAN	TESTER
BUILDER	MECHANIC	TRIMMER
BUSINESSMAN	PILOT	TRUCKER
CLOWN	POLICEMAN	WORK
COWBOY	POLITICIAN	
DINOSAURS	PORTER	
DOCTOR	PREACHER	
DREAMER	PUPPETTER	
FARMER	REINDEER	
FIREMAN	ROCKETS	
FISHERMAN	SCHOOL	

If you love

Oh, Yes I Can

then you will also love

Jelly Bean Soup and Grilled Candy Sandwiches

By Michael T.

Pictures by Joe Santoro

A Children's Book About Healthier Eating

ISBN-10: 098572675X * ISBN-13: 978-0985726751
Available through: Amazon.com, Ingram, Baker & Taylor,
Barnesandnoble.com, and Everywhere Fine Books are Sold

Upcoming releases by:

Michael T.

Illustrated by Joe Santoro

The 5 Rs:
Reading, 'Riting, 'Rithmetric, Respect & Responsibility

How Tall Is God?

Made in the USA
Lexington, KY
22 August 2018